Strangers' Bread

Nancy Willard

Strangers' Bread

Illustrations by
David McPhail

Harcourt Brace Jovanovich
New York and London

Library of Congress Cataloging in Publication Data

Willard, Nancy.
  Strangers' bread.

  SUMMARY: On his way to deliver a loaf of bread,
Anatole meets four hungry strangers.
  I. McPhail, David M. II. Title.
PZ7.W6553St   [E]   75-41361
ISBN 0-15-281750-6

First edition
B C D E F G H I J K

For Beth,
to whom bread is no stranger

Better than watching television or going to the Saturday matinee, Anatole liked to sit on the front steps of Mrs. Roscoe's corner store and watch the delivery trucks unload.

On Tuesdays, the Freihofer's truck brought coffee cake and cinnamon rolls.

On Wednesdays, the Boar's Head Provisions truck brought canned hams.

On Thursdays, the Nabisco truck brought saltines and nifty little cookies.

On Fridays, the Löwenbräu truck brought beer.
The truck from Gilbert's dairy came every day.

Anatole came every day, too, and he brought his wagon, in case he should be asked to make deliveries, for there are always people who suddenly need a gallon of milk or a jar of pickles and who don't wish to walk out for it.

For example, Mrs. Chiba. She was eighty years old, and she called up Mrs. Roscoe and said, "Is Anatole sitting on your front steps? I need a loaf of Russian pumpernickel and I need it fast. My grandchildren are coming over this afternoon."

Mrs. Roscoe pressed her face to the window, between the cigar boxes on display, and bawled through the glass, "ANATOLE, ONE RUSSIAN PUMPERNICKEL GOES TO MRS. CHIBA'S. RIGHT AWAY. O.K.?"

"I want it sliced," said Mrs. Chiba's voice from the telephone.

Anatole didn't say O.K. right off. He thought of the road to her house. He thought of himself walking to the end of all the shops, past fields of chicory and fields of clover, past a swamp, past a place of many trees. Bees tagged after him, always. The mosquitoes tagged after the bees. And the road was all uphill.

On the other hand, Mrs. Chiba might be frying up potato chips in a big pot of hot oil on the stove, and then she would give Anatole a bag of fresh chips. Or she might be baking a blueberry pie, and then she would give him a piece of warm pie. One day when she wasn't cooking anything, she gave him an elephant, carved from ivory, so tiny that he could have carried it home in his ear.

Anatole thought of all these things, and then he said, "O.K."

So Mrs. Roscoe fetched a loaf of Russian pumpernickel from the showcase, and she tucked it in the slicing machine. Snip, snap! It smelled magnificent. Then she dropped the bread in a bag and laid it in Anatole's wagon.

With the bread in his wagon, he set out.

He passed the shoe repair shop. He did not forget to salute the black cat painted on the window with one paw waving back.

He passed the beauty parlor and the taxi stand.

He passed the Episcopal church. He walked very quietly past the gravestones in the front yard.

And then he started past the fields of chicory, up the long hill to Mrs. Chiba's house.

Suddenly he saw a fox coming toward him. The fox was sniffing the air and carrying a bundle of clothes on a stick.

"Top of the morning to you," said the fox.

"And to you," said Anatole.

"You wouldn't like to help a poor starving poet, would you?" said the fox, pointing to himself.

"What do I have to do?"

"A little slice of that bread you're carrying would do wonders for me," said the fox.

"I'm taking that bread to Mrs. Chiba. It's for her grandchildren," said Anatole.

"Oh, just one little slice?" begged the fox. "I'll write a poem to make them forget they ever wanted bread. Grandchildren cannot live on bread alone."

Anatole hesitated. *Surely,* he thought, *one slice won't be missed.*

"Well, just one slice then."

"Thank you," exclaimed the fox, tearing open the package. "By the way, could you give me a lift up the hill? If you ever get to Fox Hollow and need a place to stay—"

"It's all right," said Anatole. "Hop in."

So the fox stepped into the wagon, and together they set off past the fields of chicory. The bees hummed after them. Presently they came to the fields of clover.

"Look," said the fox with his mouth full. "Here comes a rabbit."

Sure enough, a rabbit in a black gown with a black book under his paw was loping toward them.

"Top of the morning to you, Reverend Rabbit," called the fox.

"Good morning," said Anatole.

The rabbit stretched up and laid one paw on Anatole's head.

"Tell me, child, wouldn't you like to help someone whose only wish is to make the world a better place?"

"What do I have to do?" asked Anatole.

"I've been fasting for two weeks, and I need a good supper," said the rabbit. "Could I not have a slice of that bread you're carrying?"

Anatole hesitated. But who among us does not want to see the world a better place? On the other hand, if he did not deliver the bread, there would be no more bags of chips or pieces of warm pie or astonishing elephants.

The rabbit read his thoughts.

"Only one small slice," he whispered.

"All right," agreed Anatole. "One slice."

The rabbit opened the package and wriggled his nose for joy.

"Do you think," he said, "you could give me a lift up the hill? I've walked halfway round the earth, and I must catch my rest where I can find it."

He can't weigh much, thought Anatole. So he said to the rabbit, "Hop in."

So the rabbit hopped into the wagon, taking care to sit as far from the fox as he could, and the three set off, past the fields of clover. The rabbit weighed very little, but he jumped about a good deal. He read from his book as he ate, and as he read, he nodded to himself and waved his paw. Anatole found it hard to keep the wagon steady.

He was about to mention this when the fox
pulled a harmonica from his bundle and began to
play such splendid music that the flowers and trees
along the road bent forward to listen. And Anatole
found he didn't mind the rabbit's bobbing about. He
seemed to be part of the music.

Presently they came to the swamp.
"Say," whispered the fox, munching. "I've never
seen anyone like that fellow."
They all looked up. A sheep with enormous
horns and silky hair the color of sand was trotting
briskly toward them.

"Your music is divine," bleated the sheep.
"Simply divine."
The rabbit put down his book.

"Who are you?"

"I'm a Barbary sheep," said the sheep.

"Didn't we meet once at a zoo?" asked Anatole, racking his brain, for the face looked familiar.

"Tra-la-la," sang the fox.

"Leave them alone
and they'll come home
leaving the cage behind them."

"Ask me no questions, and I'll tell you no lies," said the sheep. "I'm frightfully hungry. I'll do anything for a slice of that bread you're carrying."

In the silence that followed, the Barbary sheep looked very big to Anatole—big enough to smash the wagon with one elegant hoof.

"Well, I guess one more slice won't be missed," he said, though this time he was quite sure it would be.

The Barbary sheep grabbed *two* slices and ate them in a gulp.

"Is there room for me in your limousine?" she cooed. "If you knew what I've been through—"

"Hop in," said Anatole.

So the Barbary sheep hopped into the wagon, and the four of them set off, past the swamp. The sheep was heavy, and Anatole's arms ached. The fox sang "Old MacDonald Had a Farm." The sheep couldn't carry the tune, but she beat time with her hooves, which made the wagon buck terribly.

Anatole was about to mention this when the sheep said in a thick voice (for she was chewing), "I do love a good jig, and I'm so deaf. At my age, to hear anything is a pleasure."

So Anatole hadn't the heart to say keep still. *After all,* he thought, *when I'm having a good time, I don't like people telling me not to.* But what would he tell Mrs. Chiba? He would tell her that a fox and a rabbit and a sheep ate up the bread, and she would say, "Well, why did you let them?" And he didn't know why, only he did.

The fox started playing "Row, Row, Row Your Boat."

Now they were passing the place of many trees. Suddenly the bees stopped humming, and the mosquitoes disappeared.

"I hate to interrupt," whispered the rabbit, "but is that a bear?"

They all stared straight ahead.

A bear was dancing toward them.

"Little brothers," called the bear, "can you tell me the way to London Town?"

"Never heard of it," said the Barbary sheep nervously.

"I'm pretty sure it's not in this neighborhood," said Anatole.

The bear shambled up to the wagon, panting.

"Oh, but I've been walking for miles and miles, and if I don't find it pretty soon, I shall miss my daughter's wedding. That's what comes of going off to fight wars. You're never at the right place at the right time."

And without so much as a by-your-leave, he picked up the rest of the bread and ate it.

"Is this the bus? Is there room for me?" asked the bear. "Of course there is. Always room for one more."

And he sat down in the wagon.

And then it wouldn't budge. Anatole wanted to cry. Instead, he turned to the animals.

"Look," he said, "I'd like to pull you up the hill, but to tell you the truth, I'm exhausted."

The bear jumped out at once.

"Of course you are. Why didn't I see it at once? Out of the wagon, brothers, and we'll pull the boy. One good turn deserves another."

So Anatole climbed into the wagon, and the bear took the rope in his paws, and the sheep took hold of the bear, and the rabbit took hold of the sheep, and the fox took hold of the rabbit. And together they pulled Anatole to the top of the hill.

When they reached the path that led to Mrs. Chiba's house, Anatole said, "Stop. Thanks very much."

"Don't mention it, little brother," said the bear, and he lumbered off through the trees.

"Quite all right. Top of the morning to you," said the fox, and he darted into the blueberry bushes across the road.

"God bless you," said the rabbit, and he hopped across Mrs. Chiba's yard and was gone.

"A pleasure to meet you," said the Barbary sheep. "If you meet a man with a rope, don't tell him you saw me." And she galloped on down the road and out of sight.

Holding the empty bag, Anatole walked slowly up the path to Mrs. Chiba's house. *No use lying,* thought Anatole. *The truth is best, even when it sounds like a lie.* He knocked on the door. Mrs. Chiba answered it.

"You're here just in time. My grandchildren are coming in ten minutes." And then she added sadly, "The truth is, it's my bread and raspberry jam they come for, not for me."

Anatole handed her the bag and she peered inside.

"Why, where's the bread?"

"It—it was eaten," said Anatole.

"Who ate it?"

"A fox, a rabbit, a Barbary sheep, and a bear," said Anatole.

"Not a little boy?" asked Mrs. Chiba.
Anatole shook his head.
For several minutes there was silence between them.

"Well," said Mrs. Chiba at last, "live and learn. We'll eat the jam without the bread. Come in for a little snack, won't you? I should have ordered two loaves. My mother always said, 'If you have two loaves, give one to your friends.'"
Anatole smiled.

"And if you have one loaf, give it to your strangers," he said.